With Love,
Nancy, Erin & Tara Strakaleitis

For Anna, my sweet banana

Balzer + Bray is an imprint of HarperCollins Publishers.
Nose to Toes, You Are Yummy! Copyright © 2015 by Tim Harrington
All rights reserved. Manufactured in China.

ISBN 978-0-06-232816-8

The artist scanned his pencil-on-paper drawings and used Adobe Illustrator to create the digital artwork for this book.
Typography by Dana Fritts
15 16 17 18 19 SCP 10 9 8 7 6 5 4 3 2 1 ❖ First Edition

NOSE TO TOES, YOU ARE YUMMY!

by Tim Harrington

Balzer + Bray

An Imprint of HarperCollinsPublishers

Wave your
hands, hands, hands!

Tap your
feet, feet, feet!

Tug your ears, ears, ears!

They're all so neat, neat, neat!

**Touch your
nose, nose, nose!**

Blink your

eyes, eyes, eyes!

Open and
closed, closed, closed!

From your
kissy, kissy lips!

To your big, big tummy!

I think every little bit of you is yummy, yummy, yummy!

I think every little bit of you is oh so right.

I want to hug and snuggle you oh so tight.

From the cock-a-doodle-doo!

To the snore, snore, snore!

**Every time I look at you
I want more, more, more!**

Learn to do the
YUMMY DANCE!

 Get ready...

 Wave your hands

 Tap your feet

 Tug your ears

 Shrug your shoulders

 Touch your nose

 Blink your eyes

Blow kisses

 Stick out your belly

 Yum! Yum! Yum!

 Pat all over

 Hug and twirl

 Cock-a-doodle-do!

 Fall asleep

 Jump around

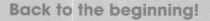 Back to the beginning!